Cave Kids

Written by
Jane Clarke

Illustrated by
Morgan Swofford

Mrs Rock stuck her head out of the cave.

"Dinner time!" she called.

Dug and his sister Trogla dropped the flints they were chipping into arrow heads and rushed to the fire pit. Their pet wolf, Howler, followed them, licking his fangs.

Mrs Rock pulled a clay pot off the embers.

"Roast mammoth!" she announced proudly.

"Yum, Yum!" gurgled baby Lava, bashing her toy club on the ground.

Dug and Trogla looked at one another.

"Mammoth again!" they groaned.

Dug tore off a lump of rubbery meat. A long, stringy mammoth hair stuck in his teeth as he chewed.

"Where's Dad?" Trogla asked, feeding bits of mammoth to Howler while Mum's back was turned.

"He's digging a pit near the river. He's hoping to ambush a mammoth when it goes to drink." Mrs Rock smiled. "If he's successful, we can eat fresh mammoth every day!"

Dug and Trogla sighed. It would take ages to eat a whole mammoth!

Roast mammoth, mammoth stew, mammoth curry, mammoth burger, mammoth pizza, sweet and sour mammoth … there was no end to what Mum could do with a mammoth.

"We have to fill in that pit!" Trogla whispered as Dad came home, covered in mud and carrying his stone tools.

"It's a full moon tonight," Dug murmured. "We'll do it while everyone's asleep."

As soon as the cave echoed with Mum, Dad and Lava's snores, Dug and Trogla leapt out of their hay beds.

They threw furs around their shoulders and crept past the glowing embers of the fire pit, out into the night.

Howler trotted along beside them, keeping a look-out for sabre-toothed tigers.

The standing stones cast creepy moonshadows as they passed, and a big elk bolted when it caught sight of Howler.

"Over there!" Dug pointed to a heap of loose earth near the river bank. They hurried towards it.

"This is Dad's pit," Trogla agreed. "I can see the grid of branches he's concealed it with … "

"Something's fallen into the pit!' Dug pointed to a hole in the branches.

A high trumpeting noise came from the depths of the pit. Cautiously Dug peered over the edge, into

the darkness. In the bright moonlight, he could see a tiny mammoth.

"It's a mammoth!" he whispered. "But it's only a baby … "

"We have to rescue it before its mother comes to find it and falls into the pit as well," Trogla said thoughtfully.

The ground began to shake. There was a loud *haroooomph!* A dark shape with long pointed tusks charged towards them.

"Too late!" Trogla gasped. "It's the mammoth's mum!"

"There's no time to run!" Dug shouted. "Jump in the pit!"

Whump! Trogla, Dug and Howler landed in the bottom of the pit.

There was a shower of sand and twigs as the mother mammoth skidded to a halt at the edge of the pit above them.

Howler wagged his tail at the baby mammoth. The baby mammoth tried to hide behind Dug.

"We're stuck here until Dad checks the pit in the morning," Trogla sighed.

There was another *harrromph!*

Dug, Trogla and Howler flattened themselves against the pit walls as the mammoth mother knelt down at the edge and lowered her huge hairy head.

The baby stretched its trunk out to hers. The two tusks twined together and the mother mammoth began to pull the baby out of the pit.

"Grab a tusk!" Dug yelled. "She won't injure us now she's got her baby back."

Wheee! Dug and Trogla swung out of the pit on the mother mammoth's tusks.

They dropped to the ground and watched as the the mother gently stroked her baby with her trunk.

"That's so cute," Dug murmured.

"I'm so relieved we don't have to eat them!" Trogla smiled, as the mother and baby stomped off into the night.

"Arooo!" Howler howled from the bottom of the pit.

"You're safe there, Howler. We'll get you out tomorrow," Dug reassured him. Howler's ears drooped. He lay down with his head on his paws and gave a deep sigh.

Dug and Trogla hurried back to the cave and pretended to be asleep when Dad got up early to check the pit.

"You'll never guess what I found in the pit!" he told Mum and Dug and Trogla.

"A mammoth?" Trogla asked innocently.

"A wolf!" Dad said. "A wolf called Howler."

Howler ran up to them, wagging his tail in delight.

"I know you must be disappointed not to have any fresh mammoth," Mum said. "But the good news is, I still have three frozen ones in the glacier. It's mammoth pancakes for breakfast, everyone!"

Dug and Trogla looked at one another and groaned.

"Yum! Yum!" gurgled Lava.